Readers Love the
Date with Destiny Adventures!

"Like an interactive episode of *Sex and the City*.
I read it nine times!"
—Erin, 28, publicist

"Everything I look for in a good book:
adventure, romance, and dozens of fantastically
good-looking UPS men."
—Melissa, 24, teacher

"At last! A chance to make stupid dating mistakes
without suffering any real-life consequences!"
—Debbie, 27, florist

"Finally! A chance to have cheap meaningless sex
without suffering any real-life consequences!"
—Julie, 32, architect

**Don't miss these future
*Date with Destiny Adventures!***

....

MY WHITE HOUSE INTERNSHIP by Miranda Clarke

PROM NIGHT A.D. 2120 by Miranda Clarke

HELP! I'M TRAPPED IN AN AARON SPELLING TEEN
    DRAMA! by R. A. Klofine

A SURPRISE VISIT FROM AUNT FLO by Miranda Clarke

THE MARTINI CHRONICLES by Miranda Clarke

DOCTOR, THAT TICKLES! by R. A. Klofine

JOURNEY TO THE BOTTOM OF BEN AFFLECK
    by Miranda Clarke

AUNT FLO STRIKES AGAIN
    by Miranda Clarke

I KNOW WHO YOU DID LAST SUMMER
    by R. A. Klofine

ESCAPE FROM FIRE ISLAND!
    by James H. English

SOMETHING CASHMERE THIS WAY COMES
    by R. A. Klofine

AUNT FLO: FIRE WALK WITH ME by Miranda Clarke

.

A DATE WITH DESTINY ADVENTURE

NIGHT OF A THOUSAND BOYFRIENDS

By Miranda Clarke

Illustrated by Pamela Hobbs

QUIRK BOOKS

PHILADELPHIA

Copyright © 2003 by Quirk Productions, Inc.

All rights reserved. No part of this book may be reproduced in any form without written permission from the publisher.

This is a work of fiction. All incidents, names, and characters are the products of the author's imagination. (Except, of course, for John Cusack and Brad Pitt, who are both far dreamier than any character this humble author could dare to imagine.) Any other resemblance to actual persons or events is purely coincidental.

Library of Congress Cataloging in
Publication Number: 2002094334

ISBN: 1-931686-35-1

Printed in the United States

Typeset in Benguiat Gothic

Designed by Susan Van Horn

Distributed in North America by Chronicle Books
85 Second Street
San Francisco, CA 94105

10 9 8 7 6 5 4 3 2

Quirk Books
215 Church Street
Philadelphia, PA 19106
www.quirkbooks.com

NIGHT OF A
THOUSAND
BOYFRIENDS

WARNING!!!!

Reading these pages in consecutive order would be like watching *Memento* and *Sliding Doors* spliced with outtakes from *Run Lola Run* by way of—well, let's just say it would be pretty damn confusing!

Instead, begin on page 1, and follow the instructions at the bottom of each page. These instructions will guide you through many adventures and decisions. Each choice has the potential to bring you success or disaster—so think carefully!

Choose wisely, and you could end up with the love of your life. Choose poorly, and you could end up on the Internet, in a series of lurid photographs that would make your mother blush.

Anything's possible—and it's all up to you!

So it's 7:00, Friday night, and David Ryder still hasn't called.

This does not make sense. Five days ago, you met David in a Barnes & Noble. *He* was the one who started the conversation. *He* was the one who complimented the novel you purchased. *He* was the one who asked for your phone number.

And now, nearly a full week has passed, and *he still hasn't called.*

"Guess I'm staying home tonight," you decide.

Your roommate, Marcy, is delighted. Marcy stays home *every* night—and if she had her way, *you'd* stay home every night, too. Whenever you're single, Marcy acts like your best friend. But whenever you're dating, she gets all jealous and grouchy and irritable.

"He's probably some asshole just looking to get laid," she says. "You're better off staying home."

"All right," you tell her. "I will."

Then, much to your surprise, the phone rings.

Turn to page 14.

"You're so lucky to have season tickets!" you exclaim. "I just love baseball."

"That's great!" Brian exclaims. "Do you think we'll make it to the playoffs?"

You decide it's best to play it vague. "Sure," you tell him. "With the right kind of . . . um . . . you know, pitching, I think we could do really well."

Brian seems puzzled by your remark. "Pitching?" he asks. "We've got the two best pitchers in our division. It's our *hitting* that we need to work on."

Ouch—looks like you struck out with that topic! Maybe it's time to stop bullshitting him and start talking about something you really understand.

If you ask if he likes to watch General Hospital, *turn to page 131.*

If you mention that your last boyfriend also drove a BMW, turn to page 35.

"I'm sorry," you tell Robert, "but I've already made plans. Can we get together later in the week?"

"Sure, that sounds good," he says, but you can hear the disappointment in his voice. "I'll call you."

As soon as you hang up the phone, Marcy starts raving about the great time you'll have together. "There's so much we can do," she says. "I've just written a new batch of poems—we could light candles and read them to each other! Or we could get into our pajamas and use the Ouija board! Or we could—wait, I know—"

Marcy runs into her bedroom and emerges with a battered videocassette of *When Harry Met Sally*, a movie she has watched once a week for the last twelve years. "I just saw it last Tuesday, but we can watch it again if you want."

If you want to light candles and read poetry to each other, turn to page 9.

If you put on your pajamas and use the Ouija board, turn to page 21.

If you decide to watch When Harry Met Sally, *turn to page 58.*

You write your phone number on a bar napkin, and Pete says he'll wait ten minutes before calling you. When you return to your table, Robert Levine doesn't even ask what you forgot at the bar. He simply resumes the conversation where he left off and provides myriad details about something called Form IG755.

The ten minutes pass slowly, but finally your cell phone starts ringing. You glance over at the bar and see Pete on the house phone, waiting for you to pick up. "Excuse me for just a moment," you tell Robert.

But just as you press Talk, the mirror above the bar shatters in an explosion of broken glass, and the sound of gunfire fills the restaurant. "Everybody down!" a man is shouting. "Get down on the floor, *now!*"

Turn to page 61.

"I'm pretty sure it's Levitt," you say.

The host escorts you to a table near the window. The young man waiting for you has the chiseled good looks of a hetero GQ model. He's dressed in a charcoal-gray three-button Prada suit (you're always a sucker for flat-front trousers), but your eyes are immediately drawn to his smile, which is warm, sincere, and more than a little bit crooked.

He stands and shakes your hand. "I'm so glad you could come—it's great to finally meet you. Isn't this place unbelievable?"

Before you even sit down, you're already discussing the best new restaurants of the last six months—and it sounds as if your date has been to them all.

Turn to page 47.

Personal safety is more important than money. You hail a taxi and hope to find an ATM closer to the restaurant.

On the way to Corazón, however, your taxi hits a nasty patch of cross-town traffic, and you pass the time by reading a newspaper left behind in the back seat. The front page headline screams HOLLYWOOD HUNKS! and you discover that Brad Pitt and John Cusack are filming a movie in your neighborhood. But it's a smaller article that really captures your attention:

RESTAURANT BANDITS STRIKE AGAIN!

Last night, patrons at the exclusive gourmet restaurant Hikaru were terrorized by twin brothers Larry and Joe DeVito, better known as the Restaurant Bandits. In the last month, the bandits have robbed nine of the city's most exclusive restaurants—and have always used innocent hostages to evade police. To date, none of their hostages has been recovered alive.

You shudder at the thought of being taken hostage, but there's not much time to worry about it—your taxi has just arrived at Corazón. The fare with tip comes to ten dollars, which leaves you with exactly ten bucks.

And since there's no ATM anywhere in sight, you decide to hurry inside.

Turn to page 101.

Three days later, you have your monthly therapy appointment with Dr. Susan Taylor, and you tell her all about your adventure with Pete.

"So let me get this straight," Dr. Taylor says. "This guy was handsome?"

"Very," you say.

"And he taught art to elementary school children."

"That's right."

"And he saved the life of a rabbi by offering himself as a hostage."

"Correct."

"And he volunteered with Special Olympics on the weekends."

"Also correct," you tell her.

"But when Pete asked you out on a date, you turned him down because—"

You shrug. "I guess I'm just picky."

"Perhaps," Dr. Taylor says. "Or perhaps you're an imbecile." There's a long silence after that, and your therapist scribbles some notes on her pad.

THE END

You sit down at the bar, and before you can even order a drink, an oily stockbroker in a shiny suit oozes onto the stool beside you. He reeks of alcohol and slurs his speech: "Baby, you must be from outer space, because your ass looks out of this world."

It's one of the worst pick-up lines you've ever heard, and you tell him so. Then you walk to the far end of the bar and take another seat.

Turn to page 16.

You light some votive candles, and Marcy ducks into her room for a stack of notebooks. "I just finished a new cycle of poems about Clemens," she says.

Clemens was Marcy's one-and-only boyfriend. They broke up five years ago, and now Clemens works as a stunt coordinator in Los Angeles, where he dates a bosomy young actress with a bit role on the newest WB teen drama.

You sit down on the couch, and Marcy stands in the center of the room. "These are in memory of Sylvia Plath," she begins.

Turn to page 34.

"Dinner sounds great," you tell him. "What time?"

"Eight-thirty," Robert says. "I'll see you there."

After you hang up the phone, you spend twenty minutes trying to soothe Marcy's feelings. "Great, fine, just blow me off," she says. "But don't call me later if you wind up getting into trouble. I'm not going to bail you out."

This is not a concern. You've never asked Marcy to bail you out of a situation, ever.

But that doesn't matter—it's almost 7:30, and if you don't start getting ready, you're going to be late!

Turn to page 27.

You know you'll have better luck on the dance floor, so you head out to the center of the club and start working your moves. It doesn't take long before a cute girl dressed in skin-tight, low-waisted jeans starts dancing alongside you.

"I'm Danni!" she shouts.

You manage a wave but don't really feel like talking. You're so hungry you can barely think, and you realize that dancing is a bad idea. Your blood sugar is hitting rock bottom, and you're starting to feel dizzy. But the dance floor is so crowded, you can't escape. You try pushing your way through the crowd, but you're not even sure which way you're going.

"Hey, are you all right?" Danni asks. "You don't look so good."

And then, all at once, everything goes black.

Turn to page 111.

At the bar, you immediately notice a tall man with long black hair dressed in a leather jacket. Hanging from his shoulders are a pair of busty blond teenagers dressed like extras from a *Conan the Barbarian* movie. But when he sees you approaching, he shrugs them off and walks over.

"I'm Chaz," he says, and shakes your hand. "Can I buy you a drink?"

"What I'd really love is some food," you confess. "I haven't eaten since lunch."

Chaz calls over the bartender and says, "Get us a plate of empanadas and two shots of Jack Daniel's."

As the bartender pours out the drinks, you tell Chaz that you don't want any Jack Daniel's.

"The whiskey's for me," he explains. "You said you wanted food."

Then he slams both glasses as if they're filled with tap water and grins at you. It's the kind of smile you'd notice from all the way across the bar.

Turn to page 109.

A man asks for you by name, and introduces himself as Robert Levine. "Your sister Jane gave me your number," he says. "I hope she mentioned me."

In fact, your sister has been raving about this guy for months. "He's a total sweetheart," Jane keeps telling you. "Every woman in our office has a crush on him. And I just know you guys would hit it off."

"Sure," you reply, in your best phone flirty voice. "I think Jane mentioned you."

"Well, I've got a bit of a problem," Robert says. "My mother was supposed to fly in from Florida tonight, and I'd made dinner reservations at Corazón."

"Corazón?" you ask. "That place has a three-month waiting list. It's supposed to be out of this world!"

"I know," he says, "but my mother's flight was canceled, so she can't make it. Now I know it's pretty rude for me to call at the last minute, but I was hoping you could join me."

You're not sure what to do. On one hand, a table at Corazón is hard to turn down—every food critic in the city has been raving about it for weeks. On the other hand, your roommate, Marcy, has overheard your end of the conversation and already looks betrayed. If you go out tonight, she's going to be pissed.

If you agree to meet Robert for dinner, turn to page 10.
If you ask for a rain check and stay home with Marcy, turn to page 3.

Brian lives on the top floor of the building, in one of the penthouse suites—but when you arrive at the door, he asks if you'd mind waiting in the hallway for a few moments.

"My place is a mess," he says. "I just want to make sure there aren't any boxer shorts lying around."

You file away a mental note for later—*boxers, not briefs*—and wait patiently. But after five minutes, you start to wonder what's going on. After all, if Brian's apartment is such a mess, why did he invite you over in the first place? What could he possibly be doing in there? Hiding something? Using the bathroom? Mopping up blood?

At long last, the door opens. Brian looks winded and out of breath.

"Sorry about that," he says. "It's much more presentable now. Come on in."

Turn to page 127.

The bartender—a cute, clean-cut guy in a black shirt with rolled-up sleeves—sets a cocktail napkin in front of you and apologizes for the stockbroker's rude remark. "Let us bring you a drink on the house," he says. "What would you like?"

You ask for a glass of Shiraz and end up explaining your whole situation to the bartender, whose name is Pete. He's very soft-spoken and easy to talk to, and he insists there must be a reasonable explanation for Robert's tardiness.

"Well, enough about me and my problems," you say. "How long have you worked here?"

"Just for the summer," he explains. "I start teaching again next week, so this is my last night."

It turns out that Pete teaches art classes at the local high school. He specializes in watercolor and oil paint, and many of his creations have been used on book jackets and album covers.

"That's terrific," you tell him. "Do you have any here?"

He shakes his head. "But this coffee shop across town has some on exhibit," he says. "I mean, if you're really interested." You can tell he's fumbling for the right way to invite you—it's clearly awkward for him, since you *are* waiting for another date.

Turn to page 71.

"It's a tempting offer," you tell Chaz, "but I feel like dancing. I'll catch up to you later."

You head downstairs, onto the main dance floor, and pretty soon you're dancing with a cute girl dressed in skin-tight, low-waisted jeans. "I'm Danni!" she exclaims, shouting to be heard over the music. "And I love this place! Don't you?"

"It's fabulous!" you tell her.

After the night you've had, it's great to finally kick back and have some fun—and Danni's certainly a fun person to dance with. She seems to have practiced every goofy '50s dance that ever existed—the Monkey, the Swim, the Frug—and introduces a new move to her repertoire every few minutes or so. Dressed in a halter top and those amazing jeans, she's just sexy enough to carry it off.

You copy her movements, laughing hysterically, and pretty soon there's a large crowd of people circled around you, applauding and cheering you on.

Turn to page 41.

There's no way you can leave the hotel without taking a quick shower.

You've seen cleaner bathrooms in fraternity houses, but at least the tub itself looks safe. Unfortunately, there doesn't seem to be any soap, so you have to scrub yourself all over with Chaz's psoriasis shampoo. It has a strong, sulfuric, medicinal smell, and it leaves you feeling sanitized, if not exactly clean.

When you emerge from the bathroom, wearing your lucky black dress, you discover that Chaz is still sleeping—thank God. You slip out the door and don't look back.

Turn to page 128.

You and Marcy sit on opposite sides of the Ouija board and rest your fingertips on the pointer.

"Go ahead," Marcy says, "ask the first question."

"Okay," you say. "Will Robert call me back?"

The pointer trembles underneath your fingertips and glides toward NO.

Then, moving more urgently, it begins to spell out words: HE BAD MAN STAY HOME WTH MARCY SHE GOOD FRIEND DON'T TAKE HER 4 GRANTED.

"You're pushing it," you tell Marcy.

"No, I'm not," she insists. "I swear to God. This is so freaky!"

The pointer continues spelling out words: MARCY GOOD FRIEND GOOD POET SOON GOOD MAN WILL LOVE HER AND APPRECIATE HER INNER BEAUTY.

Marcy starts asking questions about her future, and the Ouija board offers details about a sprawling horse ranch, an Academy Awards acceptance speech, and a tempestuous one-night stand with all of the Baldwin brothers. After a while, the game gets boring, and you end up going to bed by 9:30.

But as you fall asleep, you can't help but wonder how the night might have ended differently.

THE END

"Thanks," you tell the doctor, "but I'll just call my roommate."

"All right," he says. "Glad you're feeling better."

After he's gone, you dial your home phone number. It rings several times before Marcy finally answers. "Hello?" she asks.

"I need a huge favor," you tell her. "I'm at the hospital, and I don't have any money for a cab. Can you come get me?"

"You got stood up?" Marcy asks.

"Stood up? No, I just told you, I was hospitalized!"

"Well, you don't have to start *screaming* at me! I already told you, I'm not bailing you out this time! Why don't you call your new *boyfriend* and ask *him* for a ride?"

Marcy slams down the receiver. You hang up the phone, move to the waiting area of the emergency room, and sit down in an uncomfortable plastic chair. It shouldn't be *too* long—most of your friends usually get home around one in the morning . . .

THE END

"There's a first time for everything," you tell Chaz. "I'll try it."

He uncaps the prescription bottle and gives you a small white tablet. You swallow it with a sip of water, and then he grabs your hand and pulls you onto the dance floor.

After just three minutes, the Ecstasy starts to kick in—and after five minutes, you don't even remember taking it. You just know you're at the biggest party of the century, and you start kissing every man—and every woman—who'll dance with you. You've never seen so many beautiful people before. You can't stop touching everyone's hair.

After a while, Chaz suggests that maybe it's time to go back to his hotel room—he's staying right across the street. But you're feeling too good to leave the party just yet. "This is the best night of my life!" you tell Chaz. "Our friends want us to stay here."

"We don't have to go back to the hotel," Chaz says. "We could walk over to the hotel together. Or you could follow me back to my room."

You're having a hard time understanding what Chaz is saying—but he's such a funny and wonderful and handsome man, you don't really care where you go next. On with the party!

If you go back to the hotel with Chaz, turn to page 112.
If you follow Chaz back to the hotel, turn to page 112.
If you and Chaz go to the hotel together, turn to
    page 112.

You've seen *Independence Day*, and you're no dummy—you know that aliens can never be trusted, especially aliens who are cunning enough to disguise themselves as fantastically good-looking UPS men! You bolt for the exit, elbowing the little bald man as you run past him, and hurry onto the catwalk. When you get to the elevator, however, the doors won't open!

"HELP!" you scream down to the dancers. "FOR THE LOVE OF GOD, PEOPLE, THIS ISN'T A NIGHTCLUB! IT'S A RECRUITMENT CENTER! THEY'RE ALIENS!" But the dancers seem oblivious to your presence; it's as if you're sending your voice out into a vacuum.

Xandor steps onto the catwalk, followed by the little bald man and all of the other UPS delivery men. "We have clearly misjudged you," Xandor says, "because no queen of Neptune would ever behave in this fashion." He reaches into his pocket for a device that looks like a ray gun and takes aim at your face. As you release a blood-curdling scream, Xandor explains, "We have no choice but to send you two hours back in time."

The ray gun emits a bright yellow beam, and you feel a strange, tingling sensation all over . . .

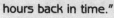

Turn to page 27.

"Excuse me," you tell Robert, "but I think I forgot something at the bar."

As you walk across the restaurant, you see that Pete is chatting with one of his customers, a bearded rabbi dressed in a dark suit and a yarmulke.

"Listen to me," the customer tells him, "you need to settle down with a *nice* girl. A girl with *substance*. Not one of these birdbrain *kurvas*."

"It's not easy when you're a bartender, Rabbi," Pete says. "Women just assume I'm a dumb, beer-guzzling jock. They don't know about my master's degree in art history. Or that I volunteer every week-end with Special Olympics—"

"Excuse me," you tell them. "I'm sorry to interrupt, but you have to help me. My date won't stop talking about tax forms. If I don't get out of here, my brain's going to turn into mush."

"Tax forms?" the rabbi exclaims. "What kind of schmuck discusses tax forms on a date?"

Turn to page 53.

In your most stern and serious voice, you tell Brian there are a couple of things you would like him to explain. "Hold that thought for just a moment," he says, and then walks out to his balcony and lights the gas grill. "This takes a few minutes to warm up, and I know you must be starving." Once the grill is lit, he goes over to the sink and washes his hands very thoroughly, as if he's preparing for some kind of invasive surgery. Finally, he sits across from you and gives you his complete, undivided attention. "All right," he says. "What would you like me to explain?"

Before you can even confess to snooping, there's a knock at the door.

Turn to page 114.

You go to your bedroom and put on your favorite outfit: a black one-shoulder Calvin Klein dress that hugs every curve without looking skanky. You picked it up for a song at a sample sale, and it's brought you luck every single time you've worn it.

After a quick primping session, you head out to the living room, dodge a hateful glance from Marcy, and leave your apartment. As soon as you get outside, you realize you only have twenty dollars in your handbag—enough for a cab ride to Corazón but not nearly enough to pay for your share of the meal. Of course, since Robert invited you, he must intend to pay for you, right?

Down the street is a dimly lit vestibule that contains an ATM. Two teenage boys are hovering outside, drinking out of bottles wrapped in brown paper bags. In your self-defense classes, you were told to avoid these kinds of situations. But, then again, you've lived in this part of the city for three years, and you've never heard of anyone getting mugged.

If you use the ATM to get money, turn to page 87.
If you hail a cab instead and worry about getting
money later, turn to page 6.

The managers' "office" is really more like a small auditorium, with thirty seats and a small podium with a microphone. The seats are filled with some of the most fantastically good-looking UPS delivery men you've ever seen, and they all start applauding when you enter the room.

"Go to the podium," the little bald man says. "They're waiting for you."

You approach the podium and speak into the microphone. "What's the big idea?" you ask. "Is this some kind of postal convention?"

A tall, strapping black man in the front row stands up. "We are not employees of the United Parcel Service," he says. "We have simply assumed this form because we know you find it aesthetically pleasing. My name is Xandor, and this nightclub is my recruitment center."

"A recruitment center?" you ask. "Who are you recruiting for?"

"The people of planet Neptune," Xandor explains. "We are looking for a queen."

Turn to page 119.

You decide it's time to take control of the conversation, so you interrupt Robert's discussion of Clause 943JL-3 and ask, "Did you hear John Cusack and Brad Pitt are filming a movie in the city?"

"I'd hate to be filing their tax returns," Robert says. "Royalties and residuals are such a bitch." Then, before you can stop him, he changes the topic of discussion to his recent business trip to Barcelona.

You should have known you were powerless to change the conversation; Robert isn't interested in anything you have to say. You sit back and let his words wash over you, and pretty soon you're fantasizing about his money again. *A trip to Barcelona would be nice, and I've always wanted to summer in Cannes. With the right hairstyle and different trousers, he wouldn't be so terrible. And Marcy would be so jealous . . .*

When Robert suggests paying the bill and going for a walk, you barely hear a word he's saying. You simply nod in agreement and follow him out of the restaurant. He doesn't hold the door for you.

Turn to page 48.

"Sorry," you tell the little bald man, "but my friend and I are busy!"

You resume your dancing but notice that the bald man doesn't stray very far—he's always just a few feet away. On several occasions, you catch him glancing in your direction and then scribbling furiously on his clipboard.

"Just ignore him, sweetie," Danni says. She starts dancing closer to you, undulating her body like Elizabeth Berkley in *Showgirls* and grinding her hips against yours.

"He keeps staring at us," you tell her. "What do you think he wants?"

Danni places her mouth against your ear. "Maybe we should get out of here," she says. "My apartment's three blocks away."

There's a coy look in her eyes, and you realize that you're being propositioned. You haven't received this kind of invitation from a woman since your sophomore year of college (and back then, you were way too scared to accept it).

If you *were* going to be with a woman, you'd want her to be someone as sexy and vivacious as Danni. On the other hand, maybe you're just too old for this sort of thing.

If you agree to go to Danni's apartment, turn to page 92.
If you use the managers as an excuse to get away, turn to page 77.

After resting for a few minutes, you and Pete walk up to the highway and wave down the first passing truck. The driver takes one look at Pete's arm and insists on driving you all the way back to the city so that Pete will receive the very best possible medical attention.

You spend the next two hours in the hospital lobby, talking to nurses, doctors, and police officers. All the while, you have the strangest sense of déjà vu, as if you've been here several times before but can't remember exactly when.

Finally, the ER doctor comes out to speak with you. Under normal circumstances, you'd find him pretty cute—albeit in a brainy, Noah Wyle sort of way—but you're so concerned about Pete, you don't even notice.

"Your friend's going to be okay," the doctor says. "There's no permanent damage to his arm, but we'd like him to spend the night anyway, just to be safe. You can visit him for a few moments, if you like."

Turn to page 104.

"We need two hostages to get past the cops," Larry announces. "Any volunteers?"

No one raises a hand, and Joe points to the rabbi. "Get over here, old timer. You're coming with us."

Then Larry spots a pregnant woman in the dining area. She's young, in her early twenties, and an obvious first-time mother. "You're coming, too," Larry tells her. "Cops *definitely* won't shoot at you."

The woman shakes her head, terrified. "I'm due in two weeks!" she exclaims. "Please don't do this to me. You can't—"

"On your feet, lady!" Larry shouts.

The pregnant woman turns to you. "Please, miss, you've got to take my place. I can't go through with this, not in my condition. You have to help me."

You feel sorry for the woman—but at the same time, you don't want to be a hostage, either. No hostage of the Restaurant Bandits has ever been recovered alive. So what will you do?

If you offer to take the pregnant woman's place as hostage, turn to page 113.

If you stay quiet and pray for her safety, turn to page 40.

In a low, trembling voice, Marcy reads:

> So are you happy now?
> With your skinny pseudo-actress girlfriend?
>   With your superficial lifestyle?
> With your empty, shallow existence?
> Is this what you really wanted?
> Is it?
> Sometimes I think you're happy
> and it makes me
>   Sick.

Marcy lowers her head, pauses, and then turns to a new page in her notebook.

Turn to page 42.

"Here's a funny little coincidence," you blurt out. "My last boyfriend drove a BMW just like this one. Only maybe it was a little newer. It had a sunroof, too."

Brian cringes, as if you've just insulted his masculinity, and you quickly struggle to make him feel more comfortable: "But listen, my last boyfriend was an asshole. He cheated on me with his dental hygienist, can you believe that? He met her while getting his teeth whitened. This guy would pay five hundred bucks for a brighter smile, but his idea of a swanky dinner was the Jack Daniel's steak at T.G.I. Friday's."

"That's terrible," Brian remarks.

"That's just the beginning!" you tell him. Just thinking about your ex-boyfriend makes you furious, and all of your hatred for him comes flooding out. "He kept all this porn hidden in a box at the bottom of his closet. I found it while he was taking a shower. It was disgusting!" You go on to describe his awful taste in music, his obsession with Tomb Raider, and his subscription to *I Can't Believe She's 18!* You even mention the time you pried open his nightstand drawer and discovered old letters from his high-school girlfriend.

And by the time you're finished, you realize that you've been parked in front of your apartment building for ten minutes—and Brian is sighing rather impatiently, anxious for you to get the hell out of his car.

THE END

"We have to steer toward the rapids," you tell Pete. "It's our only chance to escape!"

The current quickly accelerates, pulling you down the river, and you do your best to navigate the large boulders and whirlpools. Your canoe nearly topples several times—but when you glance back, you realize the bandits are way, way behind you. There's no way Larry and Joe can navigate this kind of water in a powerboat, let alone catch up to you.

Unfortunately, while you're glancing backward, your canoe smashes into a fallen tree and topples over. Pete is instantly sucked downstream, and you dive after him, grabbing him by the shirt collar.

"I'm okay, I can swim," Pete insists, but you refuse to let go, knowing very well that men with bullets in their shoulders cannot swim. It takes a good fifteen minutes of concentrated effort, but you finally make your way to the bank of the river and then collapse with exhaustion on a small, sandy beach.

Pete collapses beside you, takes your hand, and kisses it.

"Thanks," he says, nearly breathless. "I owe you one."

Turn to page 32.

You manage to shake John Cusack's hand but can't think of a single appropriate way to greet him. You've never felt so starstruck in your life.

"I met John at the Chinese restaurant down the street," Marcy explains. "We were both ordering chicken lo mein. Now what are the odds of two strangers ordering the same meal in the same restaurant at the same time? It's like—what was that movie, John? *Serendipity!*"

"It really was serendipity!" John agrees. "It's so nice just to be with a normal person, a person I can really talk to."

"And John *loves* my poetry," Marcy says. You realize that several of her poetry notebooks are stacked up on the couch. "We're going to light some candles and read a few sonnets to each other. That is, if you'll excuse us."

A few minutes later, you're lying in your bed, trying to fall asleep, but you're too distracted by the sound of John Cusack reading Marcy's poetry. You're even more distracted when the poetry reading stops—and you're forced to imagine what Marcy is doing to John Cusack on your sofa. As you pull a pillow over your head, trying to block out every noise in the apartment, you're certain you'll never understand what makes men tick.

THE END

Nine months, six days, three hours, and forty-eight minutes later, you find yourself back at the City Central Hospital—only this time you're in the maternity ward, with your knees bent, in the midst of your final contraction.

"Very good," one of the nurses is telling you. "Almost there, almost there—perfect!"

The sound of a baby crying fills the room, and your obstetrician smiles at you. "It's a girl!" she exclaims.

Dr. Brian Anderson is right by your side, squeezing your hand. "You did it, baby," he says. "It's over. You're finished!"

You barely hear a word he's saying. The last nine months have been such a whirlwind: that crazy night in the emergency room, the unexpected pregnancy, moving into Brian's apartment, the spur-of-the-moment wedding, and now this. At last, you hope to yourself, this crazy misadventure is finally coming to an end.

But when the nurse places your newborn daughter in your arms—and you see the tears of joy streaming down Brian's cheeks—you realize that your adventures together, as a family, are just beginning.

THE END

40

You can't risk your life to protect some person you don't even know. You and all of the other women remain silent, ignoring her pleas for mercy.

Then Pete steps out from behind the bar, still clutching his bleeding wound. "Take me instead," he says. "I'll be your hostage. I won't cause any trouble."

"Nah, we gotta have a woman," Larry says. "SWAT teams never shoot if there's women involved. But we'll take you instead of the rabbi."

Without further ado, Pete and the pregnant woman are marched at gunpoint out the front door, and everyone breathes a sigh of relief when they're gone.

Turn to page 45.

Next thing you know, an extremely short bald man with a clipboard emerges from the crowd. "Excuse me!" he says, shouting to be heard over the thumping bass. "The managers of the club would like a word with you!"

"I don't know the managers!" you shout back.

The bald man points toward the glass orb suspended from the ceiling. "They're watching you from the main office," he explains. "It will only take a few moments, and you'll be rewarded for your time."

The promise of a reward certainly gets your attention—after blowing your last ten dollars to get into Club Neptune, you're not sure how you'll find the cab fare to get home. But then again, you know that many nightclubs are managed by the mob. Accepting "rewards" from the "managers" might not be a good idea.

"Tell him to forget it!" Danni shouts. As the tempo of the music changes, she starts doing the Twist. "Let's keep dancing!"

If you keep dancing, turn to page 31.
If you agree to speak with the managers, turn to page 44.

"This one's called 'Prey,'" she says, and begins to read:

His hand deceived me.
His light blinded me.
His kindness betrayed me.
I am his prey.

His kiss stings me.
His style mocks me.
His betrayal burns me.
I am his prey.

Marcy bows her head and allows an eerie silence to settle in the room.

Turn to page 56.

You return to the living room as Brian is clipping the cell phone to his belt. "Sorry about that," he says. "One of the nurses had a question about a chart."

Sure, you think—*or maybe it was your wife, Elizabeth, calling you from out of town!*

"This might sound a little strange," you ask him, "but you're not married, are you?"

"Of course not!" he exclaims.

"And you don't have a live-in girlfriend or anything?"

"I'm single, and I've always lived here by myself," Brian says. "I wouldn't have invited you over if that weren't the case."

You want to believe him, but the evidence just doesn't add up. What about the name on the prescription bottle? And the pink Daisy razor? What kind of bachelor has green tea shampoo in his shower? You want to ask Brian about these things, but you can't do it unless you admit to snooping—and he probably wouldn't appreciate that.

If you confess to snooping but insist that he tell you the truth, turn to page 26.

If you try to turn up more incriminating evidence before confronting him, turn to page 93.

"I'm going to see what they want," you tell Danni. "I'll be right back."

The bald man leads you to an elevator at the rear of the dance floor. There's something very peculiar about him—he has no trouble maneuvering through the dense crowd. People just seem to disperse as he approaches and then regroup after he's passed.

The elevator doors open automatically—and when you step inside, the doors slide shut, cloaking you in absolute silence. There is no control panel, and the elevator begins rising all on its own. "What's this all about?" you ask him.

"The managers will answer all of your questions," he tells you.

Turn to page 73.

Six months later, safe and sound in your apartment, you're skimming the gossip column of the city newspaper, and you discover that local schoolteacher Mr. Peter Axelrod is now engaged to Ms. Stephanie Ashburn, a graphic designer and the unwed mother of a six-month-old baby. The column continues:

The engaged couple met under the most unusual circumstances, when two men robbed Corazón at gunpoint and took Peter and Stephanie as their hostages. "The intensity of the experience forged a deep bond between us," Pete told me in a confidential interview, "and we've been madly in love ever since."

But the story, my dear readers, gets even stranger. One week after escaping from their captors, Peter and Stephanie received a gift of ten million dollars from Albert Fitzhugh, the eccentric billionaire, who often frequented Corazón while disguised as a rabbi.

"Pete saved my life that night," Fitzhugh told reporters. "He committed a very selfless act, and I believe he deserves to be rewarded."

Peter and Stephanie will be married this June.

THE END

Dinner is heavenly: grilled salmon steaks served over rice, a mixed green salad with gorgonzola and toasted walnuts, an extraordinary bottle of Côte du Rhône, and the most delicious fudge-walnut brownies you've ever had in your life, courtesy of the valet downstairs. You're not sure if it's the wine, the spectacular view from the balcony, or simply being in the company of a good date, but you're feeling completely intoxicated. When Brian stands up to take your plate, you lean forward and start kissing him.

Over the next half hour, you both move from the balcony to the living room sofa, and then from the living room sofa to the bedroom. By this time, Brian has his shirt off, your lucky dress is hitched all the way up to your waist, and the bottle of wine is empty.

"I'm not exactly prepared for this," Brian whispers. "I don't have any protection."

And you went off the pill six months ago, after a long bout of celibacy. So now what?

If you suggest that things are moving a little too fast anyway, turn to page 88.

If you insist that Brian run to a drug store for protection, turn to page 67.

If you throw caution to the wind and unfasten his belt, turn to page 39.

After a waitress comes and takes your orders, you decide that it's your turn to carry the conversation for a while. Things are going really well until your appetizers arrive, and you ask, "So what's it like working with my sister?"

"Excuse me?" he asks.

"My sister," you tell him. "How do you like sharing an office with her?"

"I don't know what you're talking about," he says. "I'm self-employed. I told you that over the phone."

With a sinking feeling, you realize you gave the wrong name to the host, that you're sitting at the wrong table. But then again, this Levitt guy *is* pretty easy on the eyes, and the conversation is moving at a nice clip. If you stick around, Mr. Wrong could turn into Mr. Right.

So what's it gonna be?

If you fess up about the mistake, turn to page 91.
If you try to keep the act going, turn to page 57.

It's six months later, and you are no longer you.

You are Mrs. Robert Levine. You live in a nice duplex in a gated suburban community called Ebullient Meadows. You no longer have a job, since Robert makes plenty of money, and he gives you a weekly spending allowance of five hundred dollars. You can now afford everything you've ever dreamed of, including all of the clothes and jewelry and skin treatments you want. Robert works long hours at his law firm, but you find ways to keep busy; there are three different shopping malls within driving distance of Ebullient Meadows, and you visit them several times a week. You're also acquiring an extraordinary collection of Thomas Kinkade artwork.

From time to time, you think back to your old life in the city. You remember your lousy 9-to-5 lifestyle, your apartment with Marcy, and all of the awful fights you had together.

But those fights seem so long ago now. It's been so long since you've had a fight with anyone. Robert is just so good at making decisions, you never dare to disagree with him.

It's a wonderful life, and you're so very, *very* happy!

THE END

"It's definitely Levine," you say.

"Mr. Levine hasn't arrived yet," the host says, "but I can seat you at his table."

He leads you across the restaurant to a cozy table graced by a single peony in a vase. Once you're seated, a smug-looking waitress brings you a menu and asks if you'd like something from the bar.

You tell her you'll wait for your date—but after she's gone, you wish you'd asked for a basket of bread, because you haven't eaten anything since lunch, and you're ravenous.

Five minutes pass, then ten, then fifteen.

Now it's 8:50, and Robert still hasn't shown up. The waitress approaches you again. "Will your party be arriving soon?" she asks. "Because, you know, we can't hold tables all night."

"He's only twenty minutes late," you tell her.

She turns without another word and saunters across the room. You're not sure what to do next.

If you continue waiting at the table, turn to page 82.
If you give up the table and move to the bar, turn to page 8.
If you leave the restaurant, turn to page 54.

How can you turn down a foot massage from Brad Pitt? "That would be heavenly," you decide, and Brad flashes his trademark boyish grin.

"Glad to hear it," he says. As you lay down on the couch, he slips off your left shoe and cradles your foot in his lap. "Shall I pour you some wine before we begin? Maybe a glass of Merlot?"

Before you can answer, the front door opens and in walks a UPS delivery man. He's holding a device that looks like a ray gun and points it at your chest. "I can't tolerate this kind of cheating," he says.

"Cheating?" you exclaim. "I've never seen you before in my life!"

"You're ignoring the rules!" he shouts back. "You were flipping through this book and saw Brad Pitt's name and just thought you could pick up the story anywhere. Isn't that right?"

You can feel yourself blushing. "I guess I got side-tracked."

The UPS man shakes his head in disgust. "Your behavior is inexcusable," he says, and then the ray gun emits a bright purple beam of light. You feel a strange, tingling sensation all over . . .

Turn to page 1.

The next time you open your eyes, you're lying in your bed, and it's Saturday morning. You feel as if you've just awakened from the strangest dream—but when you throw back the blankets, you see that you're still wearing your lucky black dress!

You hurry out the door and walk all the way across the city, to the intersection where you found the Barnes & Noble and Club Neptune. But when you arrive, there's no trace of a nightclub anywhere. In its place is a small city park that's full of pigeons and old people and little kids playing hopscotch.

That's not the only strange thing to happen. In the weeks to come, you notice that your body is changing. Before the night at Club Neptune, you could gain five pounds just by *looking* at a cheeseburger. But lately you can eat virtually anything—pizza, pork lo mein, ice cream, *anything*—and not gain weight. Xandor's ray gun must have altered your body's metabolism so you'll always remain a perfect size 6.

You cancel your membership at the gym, enroll in a beer-of-the-month club, and eat countless pints of Häagen-Dazs. And every night before you go to sleep, you look up to the stars and say a special thank-you to your friends on planet Neptune.

THE END

"If you come around to my side of the bar," Pete explains, "there's a trap door leading down to the basement. You can sneak down there and go out the fire exit."

The rabbi immediately protests: "Are you crazy, Pete? She can't walk out on the putz! She'd break his lovesick heart and embarrass him in front of the whole restaurant!"

Pete thinks for a moment, and then he has another idea: "What if I call you on your cell phone and pretend there's an emergency? You tell your date you have to leave right away. If you're a good actress, you'll be home free."

Even the rabbi seems okay with this plan. "It's not exactly honest," he says, "but at least you won't hurt the poor *shlemiel*'s feelings."

You're not exactly sure what to do.

If you use the trap door, turn to page 118.
If you agree to have Pete call you on your cell phone, turn to page 4.

You leave Corazón and head down the street, past bars, restaurants, and boutiques. The streets are full of people, and the night is still young—anything could happen. But since ten bucks won't get you very far in this city, you make a beeline for the nearest ATM.

You insert your card and punch in your security code. Then the screen goes black. The machine makes a funny "changa changa changa" sound, as if it's preparing to spit out cash.

Then these words appear on the screen: "CARD CAPTURED. PLEASE CONTACT THIS BRANCH MONDAY TO FRIDAY DURING REGULAR BUSINESS HOURS."

"Regular business hours?" you ask. "Are you fucking kidding me?"

Hitting the machine doesn't accomplish anything. Neither does kicking it. You can't believe the luck you're having tonight.

Feeling worse than ever, you set off down the street.

Turn to page 95.

You don't know what Brian's deal is—but you've learned to trust your instincts over the years, so you head for the elevators and don't look back. It takes a good twenty minutes to walk home, but you're in no hurry because you're dreading another tense confrontation with your roommate, Marcy.

When you unlock the door to your apartment, however, you're surprised to find that the lights are dimmed, Fleetwood Mac is playing on the stereo, and there's a young man sitting next to Marcy on the living room sofa. And not just any young man, either. It's . . . it's . . .

"I'm John Cusack," he says as he stands up to shake your hand.

Turn to page 37.

Marcy turns to a new page in her notebook and continues reading:

> Are you happy with her?
> Do you think of me when you're together?
> Do you remember the times we had?
>
> Would it matter to you
> if I was
> six feet under
> and full of worms?
> Dead?

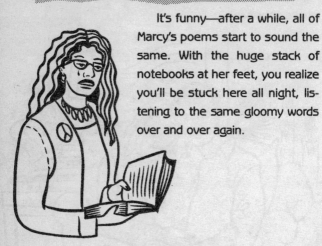

It's funny—after a while, all of Marcy's poems start to sound the same. With the huge stack of notebooks at her feet, you realize you'll be stuck here all night, listening to the same gloomy words over and over again.

Turn to page 34.

"Sister? Did I say sister?" you ask. "I'm sorry, I'm just babbling. But now tell me: how do you like being self-employed? It sounds *wonderful*."

Amazingly, you steer the conversation back on track, and soon you're both reviewing the dinner specials. All goes well for the next few minutes, until the host arrives at your table, accompanied by a young Ashley Judd lookalike in a shimmering Chloe dress.

"Alan Levitt?" she asks. "I'm Juliet. I'm so sorry I'm late."

"*You're* Juliet?" he asks, completely bewildered. "I don't understand. If *you're* Juliet, then . . . then . . ."

"It's just a mix-up," you stammer. "I know you *thought* I was Juliet, but we were having so much fun, I didn't want to say anything."

Alan, Juliet, and the host are staring at you with a mixture of pity and disgust.

"Like, excuse me, but how *desperate* can you get?" Juliet asks.

The host takes you firmly by the arm. "I'm afraid we must ask you to leave the premises."

You take a cab home, crawl into bed, and don't show your face in public for the next month. Needless to say, your roommate, Marcy, is thrilled to have you back around the house.

THE END

"Let's watch *When Harry Met Sally*," you tell Marcy.

"Excellent! I'll make popcorn!" she exclaims.

One hour later, you're sitting side by side on the sofa, watching Meg Ryan fake an orgasm in a crowded New York delicatessen.

Suddenly, the TV screen is filled with static. Marcy ejects the cassette from the VCR and discovers that it has torn from excessive viewings. "But that's okay," Marcy assures you. "I know the rest of it by heart. I'll just act it out!"

She stands and begins quoting dialogue from the film: "Men and women can never be friends! It's impossible! The sex always gets in the way—"

You close your eyes, trying to visualize Billy Crystal and Meg Ryan. But as you drift off to sleep, lulled by the cadences of Marcy's voice, all you see is the shadowy figure of Robert Levine, sitting alone at a table at Corazón. And you wonder what might have happened if you had more guts.

THE END

You and Robert are seated at a small table near the entrance to the kitchen. He explains that he's an attorney specializing in tax litigation, particularly cases involving Schedule IC504-3B. He tells you all the different reasons why Schedule IC504-3B replaced the old Schedule IC404-3A, which were both part of something called Form DL933-3X.

You glance over at the bar and catch Pete looking in your direction. He quickly averts his eyes.

When the waitress comes to your table, Robert orders a bottle of the 1981 Chateau Petrus. You don't know much about wine, but you can tell that the bottle must cost a great deal, because the manager himself comes over to serve it. "As usual, Mr. Levine, you've made an excellent choice," the manager explains. "Enjoy your meals."

Indeed, the wine is truly extraordinary. "I wish I knew more about wine," you tell Robert. "How did you learn so much about it?"

Robert shrugs. "I just order the most expensive bottle," he says. "You know the most expensive one is always the best."

Turn to page 76.

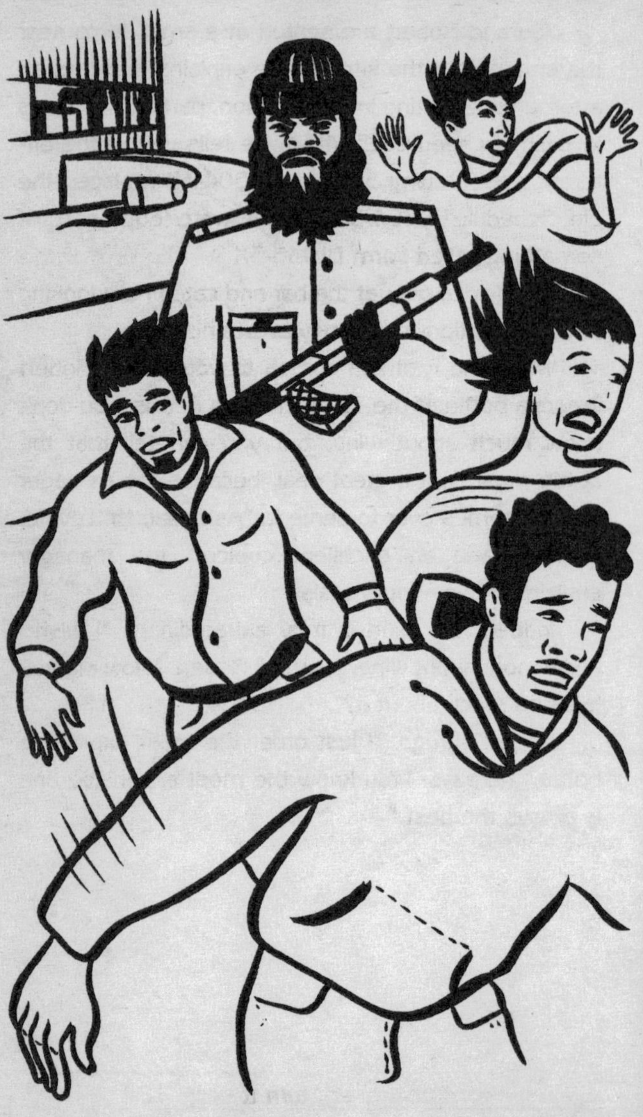

You have no idea what's happening. People are running and screaming. Robert dives to the floor, covering his head with his hands, and leaves you sitting alone at the table. Through the chaos, you glimpse a bearded man with an AK-47 rifle, spraying bullets into the ceiling.

With a shock, you realize he must be one of the dreaded Restaurant Bandits!

In the midst of the madness, you hear Pete shouting to you over the cell phone: "Get down on the floor!" he's yelling. "Knock over your table and hide behind it. Don't try to run."

You're not sure this is the best advice—the door to the kitchen is just a few feet away, and if you're fast enough, you just might make it. You're certain that Corazón must have a back door.

If you run for the kitchen, turn to page 120.
If you hide behind your table, turn to page 124.

"Grilled salmon sounds wonderful," you tell him. "Let's go."

A few minutes later, you're driving up to Kensington Terrace, one of the nicest apartment buildings in the city. A young valet hurries over and opens the door for you.

"Good evening, Dr. Anderson!" the valet exclaims.

"Hey, Teddy," Brian says. "How's your wife feeling?"

"Much better, thanks to you!" the valet says. He holds out a plate of fudge-walnut brownies covered with plastic wrap. "She made these for you. As a token of her appreciation."

Brian takes the plate. "That wasn't necessary, Teddy, but please thank her for me. These brownies look terrific."

Inside the lobby, on your way to the elevator, you ask, "What was that all about?"

Brian shrugs. "Just a routine house call. The valets don't receive any health insurance benefits, so I try to help their families if I can."

Turn to page 15.

You help Pete onto the motorcycle, then sit in front of him and wrap his good arm around your waist. "Hold on tight," you tell him, and then you gun the engine. There's no muffler on the bike, and it sounds like a thousand lawn mowers roaring to life.

Larry and Joe come running out of the house, firing their rifles. You crank the throttle, spraying gravel everywhere, and speed off down the dirt road. It's your first time riding a motorcycle, and you're surprised to find that the controls are fairly intuitive: lean left to go left, lean right to go right, twist the throttle to accelerate. You even manage to turn on the headlight.

But the bike seems to max out at fifty-five miles per hour—no matter how much you turn the throttle, you can't make it go any faster!

Turn to page 86.

"I'm sorry," you tell Brian, "but maybe I could take a rain check? After everything that's happened tonight, I just want to go home."

The doctor seems disappointed, but he smiles when you give him your phone number. "I'll call you tomorrow," he says, and you know that he means it.

You walk into the Chinese restaurant and order your favorite take-out meal: pork fried rice and hot and sour soup. But when the cashier rings up your bill, you open your purse and realize that you *still* don't have any money!

"I'm so sorry," you tell the cashier. "I just got out of the hospital, and I don't have any money, but I promise I could come back tomorrow and pay—"

"Unacceptable!" he shouts, and he snatches back your food. You feel as if you're ready to cry.

But then a calm voice behind you says, "Excuse me, but I would be happy to cover the young lady's bill."

Turn to page 98.

You race down to the dock, untie the canoe, and help Pete climb into the front seat. The river is moving swiftly, and there's no moonlight to guide you; for a moment, you start to wonder if maybe the motorcycle was a better option. But then you hear shouting from the cabin—Larry and Joe are out by the toolshed, and they realize you've escaped!

"We better shove off," Pete says, and he starts paddling despite his injury. "They're going to come after us."

Sure enough, Larry and Joe are running down to the boathouse. A moment later, you hear the roar of a powerboat engine.

Up ahead, a large island divides the river into two separate channels. On the left is a nasty patch of rapids—you're not quite sure if you can navigate them in a canoe. The safer, more calm channel is on the right.

"You're steering," Pete reminds you. "Which way should we go?"

If you steer toward the left, turn to page 36.
If you steer toward the right, turn to page 129.

"Why don't you run to the drug store around the corner," you tell him, "and I'll be here waiting for you." Brian pulls on his shirt and hurries out of the bedroom, and you roll over in his plush, queen-sized bed. It feels so good to be lying down, and you close your eyes just for a moment.

The next time you open them, sunlight is streaming through the blinds, and Brian is lying beside you. You're still wearing your lucky Calvin Klein dress, and the digital clock on the bedside table reads 10:30. Beside it is an unopened box of Trojans, still in a plastic Rite-Aid shopping bag.

"What happened?" you ask.

"It took me a while to find an all-night drug store," Brian admits. "And by the time I got home, you were out cold."

He stands up, naked except for his boxer shorts, and stretches his arms over his head—unwittingly offering a spectacular view of the finely sculpted abs and deltoids that you'd only glimpsed last night. Then Brian reaches for his cell phone and punches in a number.

"Who are you calling?" you ask.

"The hospital," he says. "I can't possibly go to work on a beautiful morning like this. I figured we could get some breakfast together and then see where the day takes us."

THE END

The next time you open your eyes, you're in the middle of an all-white room, lying in bed. Three people—a doctor, a nurse, and a police officer—stand beside you.

"What happened?" you ask.

"You're going to be okay," the doctor says. He's a handsome young man in blue surgical scrubs and bears more than a passing resemblance to Noah Wyle on *ER*.

The police officer holds up your purse. "They took the cash and cell phone but left everything else—license, credit cards, lipstick, all the important stuff."

"All things considered," the nurse adds, "you're very lucky. If the tests look okay, we can release you in maybe half an hour."

You glance at the clock on the wall—it's now 10:25, so there's no chance that Robert is still waiting for you at Corazón. Your first date in weeks, and you've already blown it.

Turn to page 108.

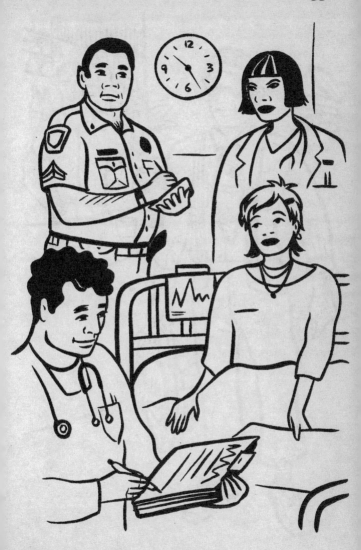

Someone taps your shoulder and says your name. "It's me, Robert Levine."

You turn around and come face to face with your blind date. He's not exactly the man you were expecting. His tie hangs three inches above his waist, his shirt is two sizes too small, and his pants are a shade of mauve not seen since high school proms of the early 1980s. You catch a whiff of his cologne, and it's like a sickly mixture of vanilla extract and mosquito repellent.

Pete politely walks to the opposite end of the bar and starts polishing empty mugs.

"I didn't think you were showing up," you tell Robert.

"I'm sorry I'm late," he says, and then he lowers his voice to a whisper: "I had to make number two."

"Excuse me?" you ask.

"I had to make number two," he says again. "I must have eaten some bad meat." Then he gestures to an empty table and says, "But I feel fine now. We can still have dinner."

You can't believe what you're hearing. Number two? Bad meat?

If you leave the restaurant immediately, turn to page 81.

If you stick around for dinner, turn to page 59.

"No, thanks," you tell Chaz. "I've had enough mind-altering experiences for one night."

"That's cool," Chaz says. "I bet you're the kind of girl who doesn't need E to party, anyway." He walks you over to a window and points to a dingy little hotel across the street; it's illuminated by a battered neon sign that reads SAMSON HOTEL—VACANCY. "I'm staying in a room on the fifth floor. Why don't we go over there and have our own private party?"

You're electrified by the boldness of his proposition—you've never received such a frank and candid offer before, although you've often fantasized about this very kind of invitation. You haven't been with a man in months, and you have a hunch that Chaz doesn't leave his partners unsatisfied.

At the same time, however, the Samson Hotel isn't exactly the Four Seasons—and who knows how many women Chaz has slept with. A thousand safe-sex pamphlets have warned you to avoid this very kind of situation.

If you accept Chaz's offer and go to the hotel, turn to page 106.

If you decline and head over to the dance floor, turn to page 18.

When the elevator opens, you step out onto a steel catwalk that's suspended one hundred feet above the dance floor. The little bald man walks across it, approaching a doorway in the large glass orb. As you follow after him, your heels clack against the metal catwalk, and you realize that something very, very strange is happening: down below you, hundreds of people are still dancing—but the only thing you hear is the sound of your footsteps!

"What happened to the music?" you ask.

"We find it distracting," the little bald man says, "so we only play it downstairs."

"How is that possible?" you ask. "This is one giant room!"

"We must hurry," he says. "The managers will answer your questions."

He approaches the door to the office and presses his hand against a glass panel. With a gentle *whoosh*, the door slides open. You have no choice but to follow.

Turn to page 28.

You travel down a long hallway lined with doors, unsure of where you're going. You accidentally open the door to Brian's office—and glimpse a messy desk covered with newspapers and medical journals—but then try the next door and find yourself in a bathroom.

While touching up your make-up, you accidentally draw a crooked line with your lipliner. So you open the medicine cabinet, hoping that Brian will have some cotton balls. What you find instead is very curious: an orange prescription bottle filled with something called Zorbitol, prescribed to someone named *Elizabeth* Anderson!

Still reeling, you yank back the shower curtain, revealing a bathtub that's lined with a dozen different bottles of shampoo and conditioner. Your eyes quickly scan the labels, which boast ingredients like lingonberry extract, seaweed kelp, ylang ylang, frankincense, and essence of green tea. And hidden behind the shampoo—looking ever so much like a smoking gun—is a pink Daisy razor.

Now you know something's up—but Brian's calling your name from the living room! Better hurry back.

Turn to page 43.

By the time your meals arrive, you've concluded that Robert is very boring—and very, *very* wealthy. Part of you finds him repulsive. He doesn't ask you a single question and talks virtually nonstop about tax loopholes, his friends at the IRS, and his extravagant spending habits.

But another part of you is fascinated by Robert's wealth. You've never met anyone your age who possessed enough money to retire. You've never met anyone who could afford to "weekend" in Paris on a whim. The more Robert talks, the more you can imagine what you'd do with all his money: Quit your job, probably. And buy a new wardrobe, definitely. You begin to think that maybe Robert isn't so bad-looking, after all: *If I bought him some new clothes and maybe changed his hairstyle, I guess I could almost enjoy sex with him. I mean, if we kept the lights off . . .*

Then you snap back to your senses. *What the hell am I thinking?!?*

You realize that Robert's words are having a strange, hypnotic effect on your brain, as if he's putting you under a spell. Maybe you need to take charge of the conversation. Or maybe you just need to end this date right now—if you go over to the bar, it's possible that Pete might help you.

If you try taking control of the conversation, turn to
     page 30.
If you go to the bar and ask Pete for help, turn to
     page 25.

"Thanks for the invite," you tell Danni, "but I'm going to keep looking for Mister Right." You try to place an emphasis on the word *Mister*, but with all the noise in the nightclub, you're not sure if she hears you.

You walk up to the bald man and tell him you're ready to see the managers.

"Excellent," he says. "Follow me."

He leads you to an elevator at the rear of the dance floor. There's something very peculiar about him—he has no trouble maneuvering through the dense crowd. People just seem to disperse as he approaches and then regroup after he's passed.

The elevator doors open automatically—and when you step inside, the doors slide shut, cloaking you in absolute silence. There is no control panel, and the elevator begins rising all on its own. "What's this all about?" you ask him.

"The managers will answer all of your questions," he tells you.

Turn to page 73.

You spend fifteen minutes waiting in line, only to learn from the doorperson that there's a ten-dollar cover charge. "But that includes free appetizers for our grand opening," he says.

You fork over the cash and hurry inside, where hundreds of people are already dancing. The main dance floor is at the bottom of a huge atrium; it's surrounded by five layers of balconies, all packed with sweaty, gyrating dancers. At the very top of the atrium, suspended from the ceiling, is a large glass orb—a model of planet Neptune, you presume.

When you finally arrive at the buffet table, you're shocked to discover that all of the trays are empty, and a caterer is unplugging the heat lamps. "You shoulda come earlier," she says. "These dancers eat like pigs."

Now what are you going to do? You could try proceeding to the bar, in hopes of convincing some desperate young man to buy you a plate of chicken fingers. On the other hand, you might attract more attention on the dance floor—and the music certainly has you primed to dance.

If you head to the bar, turn to page 13.
If you start shaking your thang, turn to page 11.

When Brian turns onto your block, you realize you still need to get something to eat—after all, it's after 11:00, and you haven't had a real meal since lunch. You point to a take-out Chinese restaurant just a few doors away from your apartment building. "I can get out there," you tell him. "Time to pick up some fried rice."

"Sure," Brian says, and he pulls alongside the curb. You're starting to thank him for the ride when Brian takes a deep breath and says, "You know, my apartment's just a few blocks from here, and I was going to go home and make some dinner, anyway. I know it's late and all, but if you wanted to come by . . ." His voice trails off. "We could grill some salmon and, I don't know, maybe catch some old *Fantasy Island* reruns."

With this last joke, his voice cracks, and you can tell Brian is nervous about inviting you to his home. Part of you knows that it's foolish to go with a stranger you've just met. But, then again, he's also the doctor who restored your health tonight. And you *love* grilled salmon . . .

If you agree to go to Brian's apartment, turn to
    page 62.
If you ask for a rain check, turn to page 65.

You use your remaining money to take a taxi home, but it's barely enough to cover the fare, and you don't have anything left over to tip the driver. As you exit the cab, you can hear him mutter the word "cheapskate" under his breath.

Life doesn't improve when you enter the apartment. All of the lights are off, and Marcy is on the couch, scribbling into her poetry notebook and watching a *Friends* rerun. An empty Häagen-Dazs container lies at her feet. She can't help but smile as you walk into the apartment.

"You're home early," she says.

"Things didn't really work out," you tell her.

"What a shame," she says, and then begins scribbling furiously into her notebook.

For some reason, you have a hunch she's writing something nasty about you.

THE END

You decide to stay at your table and give the menu a careful read from cover to cover, all the while trying to avoid the frustrated glare of your waitress.

At 9:00, the host stops by your table with a cell phone. "Excuse me," he says, "but perhaps you would like to call Mr. Levine?"

"I'm sorry," you tell him, "but I don't know his phone number."

"Then perhaps you would like to order for yourself, and Mr. Levine can order when he arrives?"

There's no way you're going to eat in such an expensive restaurant by yourself. But your remaining options are pretty limited.

If you decide to wait for Robert at the bar, turn to page 8.

If you decide to leave the restaurant, turn to page 54.

You slip into your lucky black dress, sneak out the door, and hurry home to take a shower. But even after washing yourself for twenty minutes, you still feel you've made a terrible mistake. Who knows what diseases Chaz was carrying? For that matter, who knows what diseases were in the hotel? Your body feels like a walking petri dish, and God only knows what you're contaminated with.

You call your doctor to schedule an appointment, but of course she doesn't have office hours until Monday morning. You know you can't wait that long. Late Saturday afternoon, you take a cab to the hospital, check yourself into the emergency room, and explain your situation to a handsome young doctor who reminds you of Noah Wyle. He seems slightly repulsed by your behavior but prescribes an arsenal of antibiotics.

"These should cure you of your—uh, concerns," he says.

"Thank you, doctor," you say, completely ashamed of yourself.

And it's too bad, because the doctor really is pretty handsome. Under different circumstances, it's not hard to imagine yourself hooking up with him.

THE END

After another ten minutes of driving, Larry steers the car onto a bumpy dirt road and then stops in front of a decrepit old cabin.

"All right," he says. "Everybody out."

Larry walks you and Pete around to the back of the cabin and directs you inside an old toolshed. It's filled with old, rusting gardening equipment and a large metal canister marked GASOLINE. He grabs the canister and then locks the door, trapping you inside.

"What's happening?" Pete asks.

You peer out the shed's only window and see Larry circling the shed with the canister, splashing its contents on the walls. Then he checks both of his pockets, as if searching for a match, and walks with Joe toward the main cabin.

"We've got to hurry," you tell Pete, and then you shake your wrists free of the wire cord. "They're going to burn us alive!"

Turn to page 96.

"They're coming!" Pete shouts.

You glance in the rear-view mirror and see that the Grand Marquis is gaining ground—in another minute, the car will be close enough to ram you off the road. "I can't make this bike go any faster!" you shout. "The engine's maxed out!"

"Then get off the road!" Pete shouts back. "We can't outrun them!"

On the right, you're approaching a small covered bridge that spans the river; unfortunately, it's blocked by a large sign that reads DANGER: BRIDGE CLOSED. DO NOT ENTER. In the movies, it would be perfectly sensible to crash through the bridge and emerge safely on the other side—but does that ever happen in real life?

A more realistic option might be the mountain biking trail on your left. You know the trail wasn't designed for motorcycles—especially motorcycles hurtling along at fifty-five miles an hour—but it may be your only chance to escape. There's certainly no way a Grand Marquis can follow you down it.

"What are we going to do?" Pete shouts.

If you veer toward the left, turn to page 123.
If you veer toward the right, turn to page 116.

You definitely want to be carrying money, especially if the date doesn't work out. As you approach the ATM, you summon all the skills you learned in your self-defense classes. You walk confidently, with your head held high, and the two teenagers barely seem to register your presence.

Once inside, you swipe your bank card and punch the Fast Cash button. Three crisp twenties drop out of the machine—the last sixty dollars in your checking account. As you scoop up the money, the door behind you opens.

"Grab her," someone shouts, and suddenly two strong arms reach around your waist. A heavy weight smashes against the back of your head, and you collapse to the floor.

Turn to page 68.

"Actually," you tell Brian, "things are moving kind of fast. I think the wine went straight to my head. I should probably go."

"I understand," Brian says. "Let me drive you home, then." You tell him it's not necessary, but Brian insists on it and points out that you drank most of the wine. "I'll feel better if I know you've made it home okay."

But a funny thing happens when you reach the entrance of Kensington Terrace. The valet with the fudge-walnut brownies has gone home for the evening—and the new valet looks vaguely familiar.

"Good evening, Dr. Anderson!" he exclaims. "I'll have your car here in a jiffy!"

You spend the next three minutes wondering where you've seen him before—and when he finally returns with the BMW, you realize that it's David Ryder, the same guy you met five days ago at Barnes & Noble. The same guy who promised to call you.

"Hello, David," you tell him.

David recognizes you, and his smile falters. "Oh, hey, it's you," he says. "Listen, I *was* gonna call—"

"Well, I'm certainly glad you didn't," Brian says, and then he opens your door so you can step inside his luxury BMW sedan.

THE END

"Your invitation is both an honor and a privilege," you tell the alien UPS men. "If I journeyed to Neptune, I'm sure I would make many friends and learn many fascinating secrets of the universe. But deep in my heart, I know my real home is here on planet Earth. If I were your queen, I know I would miss my human relatives, and I would never be truly happy."

At the conclusion of your speech, the UPS delivery men all rise to their feet and give you a standing ovation. "Your choice saddens us," Xandor says, "but we appreciate your candor, and we respect your decision. In fact, since you were kind enough to consider our request, we would like to give you a special gift, as a token of our appreciation."

Xandor reaches into his pocket and removes a device that resembles a ray gun. You cry out in terror, but Xandor tells you not to be afraid. The ray gun emits an orange beam of light, and you feel a warm, tingling sensation all over . . .

Turn to page 52.

"I would be honored to be your queen," you tell the aliens. "I suggest we depart for your home planet immediately."

The room is filled with cheers and applause, and your subjects usher you to a special throne at the rear of the auditorium. They strap you into the seat with harnesses, and all of a sudden, the orb-shaped auditorium begins to spin.

"Do not be afraid, your highness," Xandor says. "Thanks to our advanced interplanetary transportation systems, the return trip to Neptune will last only one Earth hour."

Through the windows of the orb, you see that you're rising straight through the ceiling of the nightclub—and heading up, up, up into outer space!

Turn to page 135.

"I think there's been a mix-up," you tell him. "I'm here to meet Robert."

"Robert? I'm Alan!" he exclaims.

You both have a good laugh over the mistake, and your timing couldn't be better. Just a few minutes later, the host shows up with Alan's *real* date: a young Ashley Judd lookalike in a shimmering clingy dress and killer stilettos.

"Please excuse me," you say. "I'm sorry about the mix-up."

You return to the host and ask if Mr. Levine is still in the restaurant. "I'm afraid you just missed him," the host says. "He left five minutes ago."

You hurry outside, hoping to catch a glimpse of him, but the sidewalk is full of people. You're too late.

Turn to page 54.

When you wake up the next morning, you're surprised to find yourself in a woman's bedroom—and then your memories of the previous night come flooding back. Danni rolls over in bed and drapes a lazy arm around your waist.

"I thought you were going to sleep forever," she says.

Whenever you've awakened in a stranger's bedroom, you've always felt an urgent need to run away as soon as possible. But with Danni, it's different. "I hope you're not in a rush to get home," she says, and then places a white envelope in your hand. "I have these tickets for tonight, and I'm hoping you can join me."

You open the envelope and find two backstage passes for tonight's Indigo Girls concert—with Ani DiFranco as the opening act! "I've got a thousand girlfriends coming to this show," she says. "I'd love for you to meet them."

Hmmm . . . a night of a thousand *girl*friends?

"It sounds fabulous," you tell Danni. "I'd love to go!"

THE END

If you return to the living room, turn to page

"I'm sorry," you tell Brian, "but I forgot something in the bathroom. Be right back."

"No problem," he says. "I'll light the grill."

As he heads onto the balcony, you return down the long hallway—only this time, instead of entering the bathroom, you duck into Brian's office and turn on the light.

It's a total mess—papers are strewn everywhere, and it would take days to sort through everything. But you do spy an answering machine on the desk, and you realize that its red "New Message" light is flashing.

Out in the living room, there's a knock at the front door. "Just a sec," Brian calls.

This is just the distraction you need—it's probably another valet with another medical emergency. In the time it takes Brian to resolve the problem, you could probably listen to the whole message.

On the other hand, the person knocking at the front door could be the solution to this whole mystery. Maybe you should return to the living room.

If you press Play on the answering machine, turn to page 133.

If you return to the living room, turn to page 114.

You leave the bank and begin walking toward home. You're not sure where you're going, but you know you need to eat something very soon. The last time you felt this hungry, you actually fainted, and you've learned not to mess with low blood sugar.

After walking for several blocks, you come to a busy intersection with a giant nightclub; it's several stories high and appears to be a renovated movie theater. The marquee reads CLUB NEPTUNE: GRAND OPENING TONIGHT! There's a long line of beautiful people waiting to get inside, and many of the women are dressed on the skimpy side. But your lucky black dress is versatile enough to get you in the door, and you're sure the bar will have food.

On the other hand, there's also a Barnes & Noble across the street. At this point, maybe you just want to grab a table at the coffee bar, scarf down a couple of cream cheese brownies, and browse through some new fiction. At this point, you're not sure you feel like meeting anyone else.

If you go into Barnes & Noble to relax, turn to
    page 105.
If you go into the nightclub to party, turn to
    page 79.
If you hail a cab and go home, turn to page 81.

You quickly untie Pete, force open the window, and help him climb out of the toolshed. He assures you that he's fine, but you notice that he's having trouble concentrating and his movements are slowing down. The loss of blood is clearly starting to affect him.

You have only a few seconds before Larry and Joe return—and with Pete's current condition, walking is out of the question. You need to get him to a doctor as soon as possible.

Fortunately, the cabin is built alongside a river. Down by the boathouse, you can see an old wooden canoe tied to a dock. You could easily get inside it and make a silent getaway.

Alternatively, there's a motorcycle parked at the head of the driveway. If you managed to start it up, your captors would hear you escaping—but you'd definitely have a huge head start on them.

If you start up the motorcycle, turn to page 64.
If you hop into the canoe, turn to page 66.

"I appreciate the offer," you tell them, "but I'm not much of an exhibitionist. You're going to have to find someone else."

"I won't take no for an answer," Reuben insists.

You're in no mood to argue with a Hollywood casting agent, so you just pick up your stuff, move to another part of the bookstore, and find a nice comfy chair to settle down in.

Pretty soon, you're completely absorbed in a literary novel by a young writer you've never heard of— someone named Diego Calatrava. It's so engrossing, you can barely turn the pages fast enough—and after an hour, when the store prepares to close, you bring the book downstairs to the cash register. This one's worth putting on the credit card.

While you're waiting in line at the cash register, a young man standing behind you observes the book that you're holding. "That's one of my favorite novels," he says. "You must have excellent taste."

Turn to page 102.

You turn around and realize that John Cusack is waiting in line behind you. He places a twenty-dollar bill on the counter and explains, "We're doing a shoot in the neighborhood, but I'm in no mood to be around Hollywood people tonight. Would you like to join me for dinner?"

You're so starstruck, you can't even speak. Even in the murky fluorescent lighting of a low-budget Chinese restaurant, John still looks Grosse Pointe Perfect! You manage to nod your head, and John carries your food to a small table for two.

For the next half hour or so, you feel as if you're living in a dream. John talks about the movie he's working on and answers every question you've ever had about all of Hollywood's biggest celebrities. "It's so nice to be around a normal person," he confesses. "You're the first woman I've met in months who hasn't tried to pitch me a movie idea."

You know he's dated every hottie in the state of California and that you'll probably never see him again after leaving the restaurant. But in spite of all that, it's still one of the best dinner dates you've ever had in your life. And when you crack open your fortune cookie, the little white slip of paper seems to say it all: MANY STARS ARE SMILING ON YOU TONIGHT.

THE END

As soon as you're inside, you understand why Corazón has earned a reputation as the city's most beautiful new restaurant. The dining room is lit almost completely by candlelight, and a glass ceiling provides a dazzling view of the night sky. The wall behind the bar is actually one large waterfall, illuminated by soft neon lights that gradually change from one color to another.

The host smiles and says, "Good evening. Welcome to Corazón."

"Hello," you say. "I'm here to meet Robert—"

Suddenly, you experience a colossal mind freeze— you can't remember Robert's last name! Robert Leonard? Robert Ludlum? You have absolutely no idea.

"Robert Lewis?" you try.

The host scans down the reservation list and then shakes his head. "I'm sorry, there's no Lewis on my list. But let's see . . . we have a table for *Levitt* at 8:30. Oh, and what a coincidence! We have a reservation for *Levine* at the same time. Does either of those sound right?"

If you think Robert's last name is Levitt, turn to page 5.
If you think it's Levine, turn to page 50.

You whirl around, fully expecting to see David Ryder, the same guy you'd met in the Barnes & Noble just five days earlier. *He* was the one who complimented the novel you purchased. *He* was the one who asked for your phone number. And *he* was the one who never actually called you.

The man standing behind you is *not* David Ryder, but you're disgusted with him all the same. "Try your line on someone else," you tell him. "I've got a terminal illness and three months to live."

"I'm serious," he says. "You're reading my first novel. I've never seen anyone reading it in a bookstore before." He shrugs. "I have to admit, it's pretty surreal. Do you like the cover? Is that why you picked it up?"

You open to the jacket flap and see a photograph of the man standing right in front of you—Diego Calatrava, the author of the book you're about to purchase. You feel like a fool. "I'm sorry," you tell him. "I didn't realize—"

"It's all right," he says. "If you're up for a drink, I'll tell you about all the lousy reviews I've had. And you can tell me about your terminal disease."

"Why not?" you tell him.

And as you hand your book and credit card to the cashier, you feel as if you've just made your best decision of the night.

THE END

You open the door and dive away from the vehicle, falling and rolling over several times, just like the stuntmen you've seen in movies. The battered Grand Marquis screeches to a halt, but you're already scrambling into the surrounding forest. By the time Larry and Joe get out of the car, you already have a fifty-foot head start.

You walk for several hours, avoiding the highways in case the bandits come looking for you. Eventually, you arrive at a small town. The local sheriff gets a city police sergeant on the phone so you can tell your story.

"They were taking Pete to a cabin in Fairfield," you explain. "You have to hurry!"

"We've already been there," the sergeant says, "and we were too late. Your friend Pete tried escaping in a canoe, but with his bad arm, he didn't have a chance. The poor kid." The sergeant pauses to sniffle and blow his nose. "Oh, if only he'd had someone to help him!"

THE END

Pete's eyes are closed when you enter his room—but at the sound of your arrival, he opens them. "You're still here?" he asks. "You really should go home. You must be exhausted."

"I wanted to make sure you were okay," you tell him. "Is there anything you need?"

"I'm fine," he says. "Please. Go home and get some rest."

Given everything you've survived together, this seems like an abrupt way to say goodbye, and you wonder if maybe he's doped up on painkillers. But there's nothing you can do except turn and walk toward the door.

"Actually," Pete says, "there *is* one thing I would like." You stop and turn around. "When I get out of here tomorrow, I'd like to take you on a *normal* first date. Without hostages and SWAT teams. Without motorcycles and canoes. Just me and you and a nice restaurant. With good security. *That's* the one thing I would like." He shrugs. "What do you think?"

If you tell Pete you'll see him tomorrow night, turn to page 130.

If you decide that tonight's adventure was more than enough, turn to page 7.

The quiet environment of a bookstore is much better suited to your mood right now—so you grab some paperbacks, make your way to the coffee bar, and order two cream cheese brownies. With every bite, your disposition improves. Sure, you didn't meet Prince Charming tonight, but any evening that ends with brownies isn't *that* bad.

As you continue reading, however, you become aware of a man and woman watching you very closely. Both are overweight, in their late fifties, and dressed in black turtlenecks. The woman is wearing horn-rimmed glasses with big, round lenses.

"Reuben, sweetheart, I must be dreaming," she says. "Do you see what I see?"

"I see it, but I don't believe it!" Reuben exclaims. "Touch her and make sure she's real!"

The woman introduces herself as Claire Rothschild and asks if you'd mind standing up for a moment. You slowly rise. "Am I in your seat or something?"

"Just turn around for us," Reuben says. "Show us the fanny."

The fanny?!? In spite of your better instincts, you spin around, and the hem of your dress twirls in a nice dramatic flourish. Everyone in the coffee bar is staring at you, and Claire and Reuben start applauding. "Sweetie, you're perfect!" Reuben exclaims.

"Perfect for what?" you ask.

Turn to page 117.

Up until now, the author of this book has refrained from objecting to the foolishness of your decisions—but this time you've gone too far! Didn't you take sex education classes in high school? Don't you know the dangers of going to cheap hotels with "importers/exporters" named Chaz? Haven't you seen those Lifetime TV movies where foolish women end up bound and gagged in a madman's garage, all because they were just trying to have a good time?

My editor cut this sermon short because *she* thinks this book is about fulfilling fantasies. *She* thinks you should be able to do whatever you want. But *I'm* the writer, pumpkin—I know what Chaz is really like. We don't call guys like him "bad boys" for nothing. What would your mother think right now?

If you follow Chaz to the hotel anyway, turn to page 112.

If you ditch Chaz and go down to the dance floor, turn to page 18.

Out on the street, a dozen SWAT team members have their rifles pointed in your direction—but Joe warns them not to open fire. "We have two hostages!" he exclaims. "And if any cops try to follow us, they're going to be *dead* hostages!"

Double-parked in front of the restaurant is a battered Mercury Grand Marquis. Larry shoves you and Pete into the back seat and then gets behind the steering wheel. Joe also sits up front but keeps his rifle pointed at you, warning you not to try anything. Within minutes, you're zipping uptown on the expressway, and pretty soon you're speeding out of the city and into the countryside. You pass a sign that reads FAIRFIELD: 15 MILES.

"Just fifteen more miles," Joe says. "And then the cabin's another two miles from the exit."

"Almost there." Larry nods.

Pete sits beside you, listening carefully but saying nothing.

And maybe it's just your imagination—but when you flex your wrists, you swear it feels as if the cord is starting to loosen.

Turn to page 125.

Once all the tests are completed, you ask a receptionist if you can borrow her telephone. The hospital is miles from your apartment, so you'll need a ride home.

But at 11:00 on a Friday night, all of your friends are out having fun. After trying half a dozen people, you finally leave a message on your sister's answering machine. "I'm at the hospital," you tell her. "And I'm out of cash. I need you to come get me."

As you hang up the phone, a man in a Brown University sweatshirt and blue jeans emerges from the ER. He's smiling at you and looks vaguely familiar, but several moments pass before you realize he's your doctor.

"I'm sorry," you tell him, "I didn't recognize you in street clothes."

"My shift just ended," he says. "How do you feel?"

"I'm fine," you tell him. "Thanks for asking."

He shows you his car keys. "I just overheard your phone message. I'd be happy to give you a ride across town, if you want."

He seems like a nice guy—and hey, he *is* a cute young doctor—but you were told in your self-defense classes never to take rides from strangers. On the other hand, your only other alternative is to call your roommate, Marcy.

If you accept the ride with the doctor, turn to page 121.
If you thank him but call Marcy instead, turn to page 22.

As you eat the empanadas, a dozen different people interrupt your conversation to say hello to Chaz. Most of these people are heavily tattooed and have enough body piercings to set off an airport metal detector. Chaz apologizes for every interruption and seems genuinely interested in you. "I don't usually see girls like you in clubs," he says. "You seem different from the others."

"Let's not talk about me anymore," you tell him. "What do you do for a living?"

Chaz claims to work for an Internet start-up, but you find this unlikely, since he also claims to work part-time at Circuit City and says he dabbles in "importing and exporting." When you ask what he imports and exports, he reaches into his pocket for a small orange prescription bottle. "Chemically engineered pleasure," he says. "One-hundred-percent pure Vitamin E. Want to give it a shot?"

You've never tried Ecstasy before, but you know it's supposed to heighten your senses and reduce your inhibitions. Which could be fun—Chaz seems like a pretty good person to lose your inhibitions around. He's not the kind of guy you'd bring home to meet your parents, but you sure wouldn't mind getting your hands on him.

If you take the Ecstasy, turn to page 23.
If you decline Chaz's offer, turn to page 72.

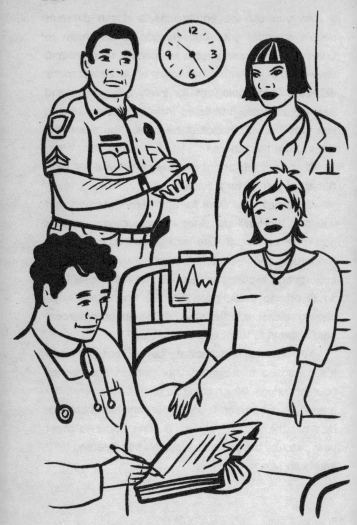

The next time you open your eyes, you're in the middle of an all-white room, lying in bed. Three people—a doctor, a nurse, and a police officer—stand beside you.

"What happened?" you ask.

"You're going to be okay," the doctor says. He's a handsome young man in blue surgical scrubs and bears more than a passing resemblance to Noah Wyle on *ER*.

The police officer shakes his head with disapproval. "You passed out on the dance floor," he explains. "In the future, if you're going to go dancing, make sure you eat something beforehand."

"All things considered," the nurse adds, "you're very lucky. We'll be releasing you in just a few minutes."

You glance at a clock on the wall—it reads 10:25, but you wish it were much later. The night has been such a disaster, you just want it to end.

Turn to page 108.

Within minutes, you find yourself undressing in Chaz's hotel room, and the next three hours rank among the most extraordinary sensory experiences you've ever had in your life. Forget Paris in springtime. Forget vintage bottles of Dom Perignon. Forget bungee-jumping and sky-diving and Six Flags roller-coasters. When it comes to sheer exhilaration—and your first experience with multiple orgasms—*nothing* beats heavily tattooed importer/exporters named Chaz.

But the next morning, everything's different. You awaken in a room with a cracked mirror on the ceiling and coffee stains on the carpet. The air is filled with the pungent stench of antiseptic. Chaz is cuddled up beside you, slack-jawed and asleep; his morning breath is atrocious, and he looks twenty years older than he did inside Club Neptune.

You feel absolutely disgusting—as if a thousand germs and viruses are crawling over your skin—and you're dying to take a shower. On the other hand, you'd really like to avoid a morning-after conversation with Chaz. Maybe you should just leave the room as quickly and quietly as possible.

If you decide to shower, turn to page 19.
If you sneak out of the room as quickly as possible,
turn to page 83.

"Take me instead," you tell Larry. "This woman could lose her baby. She's in no condition to be a hostage."

"Fine," Larry says, and then he ties your hands behind your back with a slender wire cord. "A pregnant woman would just slow us down, anyway."

"So would an old rabbi," Pete points out. He steps out from behind the bar, still clutching his wound. "Take me as your hostage, and let the old man stay here."

"All right, whatever," Joe says. "Let's just get this show on the road."

He ties Pete's wrists together with a small length of rope and then marches you both at gunpoint out the front door.

Turn to page 107.

Brian opens the door, revealing a tall, thin red-head—the very same woman from the wedding photograph on the mantel. She sees you and starts to blush. "I'm sorry, Brian," she says. "I hope I'm not interrupting anything—"

"No, of course not," Brian says, and then he introduces you to the woman. "This is my sister, Elizabeth Anderson."

Elizabeth reaches out and shakes your hand. "I'm sorry to stop by unannounced, but I left my meds in your bathroom last night. The doctors say I can't miss a single dose."

"You left a razor in the tub, too," Brian says.

While Elizabeth runs back to collect her belongings, Brian explains that his sister is having problems with her marriage and has spent most of the past week sleeping on his sofa. When she returns to the living room, Elizabeth tousles her little brother's curly hair. "You've still got a nice full head of hair, Bri," she tells him. "I don't know why you waste your money on those fancy girlie shampoos."

Then, as she opens the door to leave, Elizabeth turns to wave goodbye. "It was nice meeting you," she says. "Enjoy your dinner together."

Turn to page 46.

116

"Hang on, Pete," you tell him, and veer to the right. You crash through the DANGER sign and plunge into the darkness of the covered bridge, hoping for the best. And then, all at once, you're freefalling.

You look up and see a large gaping hole in the bottom of the bridge. Before you can even think to look down, you're underwater. The temperature is freezing, but your body's running on pure adrenaline; you grab hold of Pete and start kicking up to the surface. Bullets are splashing in the water all around you, but the current is swift, and after just a minute or two, you're out of harm's way.

"I'm okay, I can swim," Pete says, but you refuse to let go, knowing very well that men with bullets in their shoulders cannot swim. It takes a good fifteen minutes of concentrated effort, but you finally make your way to the bank of the river and then collapse with exhaustion. Pete collapses beside you, takes your hand, and kisses it.

"Thanks," he says, nearly breathless. "I owe you one."

Turn to page 32.

Claire says that she and Reuben are casting agents for the Brad Pitt-John Cusack action-comedy that's currently filming in your neighborhood. "It's a buddy movie," Reuben tells you. "With lots of action."

"And a great love story," Claire adds. "Brad Pitt falls in love with Kirsten Dunst. But we've got a mega-problem on our hands, because Kirsten's body double walked off the set today, and we have to shoot the big love scene tomorrow."

"We'll pay union rates," Reuben says. "Five thousand for a day's work. Now how many women get offered five thousand dollars just to make out with Brad Pitt?"

"Wait, hold on," you tell them. "You want me to be Kirsten Dunst's body double? We have totally different hair!"

Claire laughs at your naiveté. "Honey, nothing above your shoulders is going to appear in this movie," she says. "No one will ever have to know that it's you."

"It'll be a closed set," Reuben promises. "Just you, Brad, and the director."

Well, it's not as if you have any big plans for tomorrow—and five thousand dollars is hard to walk away from. On the other hand, there are some things you swore you'd never do for money. Is this one of them?

If you take the job, turn to page 122.
If you decline the offer, turn to page 97.

"I think I'll use the trap door," you tell them.

Pete walks over to Robert and distracts him while you sneak around to the other side of the bar. The trap door is made of heavy wood, and you need both hands to pull it open. A rickety ladder and a yawning black hole stretch below you.

"This just isn't right," the rabbi mutters into his drink, but you descend into the darkness and pull the trap door closed anyway. The basement is pitch black, and you can't find a light switch. You hold out both hands and walk around the perimeter of the room until you finally feel a doorknob.

But before you can open it, something warm and furry brushes past your ankle—and two sharp fangs sink into your skin! You throw yourself against the door, collapse into an alley, and see a huge black rat scurrying away. Blood is trickling down your ankle. You limp out to the street, hail yourself a cab, and ask the driver to take you to the emergency room.

Looks like you've made a date with a series of painful rabies vaccinations.

THE END

An image of planet Neptune suddenly appears on the wall behind you. The man who calls himself Xandor continues his speech: "We have traveled hundreds of millions of miles to reach your planet, and we have just one night to select our queen. You are by far the most perfect candidate we have seen, and we would be honored if you would serve us."

"Wait a minute!" you exclaim. "You guys are aliens? Like the green and scaly kind?"

"We can manifest ourselves in any form that your majesty finds pleasing," Xandor says. "If you join us, you will live a life of incomparable luxury. Your every wish will be our command. Your very name will be a blessing. A dozen servants will wait at your beck and call. And there is only one stipulation: You will never return to Earth again. Because of time constraints, we must have your decision immediately."

Xandor seems sincere, and the idea of being a queen has an obvious appeal. But you would definitely miss your family and friends—heck, you'd even miss Marcy! And besides, how do you know you can even *trust* these aliens? If you turn down their offer, how do you know they won't try to kill you?

If you accept their offer to be queen, turn to page 90.
If you politely decline the offer, turn to page 89.
If you don't trust the aliens and want to run for it,
     turn to page 24.

You jump up and bolt for the kitchen—and run right smack into another man holding an AK-47 rifle. "Not so fast," he says. Pete must have seen this man coming from his position at the bar, and now you wish you'd listened to his advice.

The man grabs your wrists, drags you over to the kitchen's industrial-sized freezer, shoves you inside, and locks the door. After fumbling around for a minute, you manage to find a light switch. You're surrounded by boxes and boxes of ribs, roasts, tenderloin, chicken, and chops—all of it frozen solid. The thermostat on the wall reads twenty-five degrees.

You wonder how long it will take before someone comes looking for you. Then you cross your arms over your chest, shiver, and wish that you'd worn a longer dress.

THE END

Five minutes later, you're zipping across the city in Dr. Brian Anderson's sporty BMW. You're tempted to view the automobile as a bad omen—your last boyfriend also drove a Beemer, and he cheated on you with his dental hygienist.

But Brian seems much nicer than your last boyfriend, and he acts genuinely interested in you. He asks about your job, your family, and your apartment. There are few awkward pauses in the conversation— just enough to assure you that Brian doesn't drive his patients home every night. But he makes a solid effort to keep the discussion alive. As he drives past the city's baseball stadium, he mentions that he has season tickets.

"I'm a total baseball freak," he confesses.

You don't know anything about Major League Baseball, so you don't say anything. Now the silence is beginning to feel uncomfortable. Brian switches on the radio, and you struggle to think of a conversation topic. Unfortunately, your entire knowledge of the medical profession is based on episodes of *General Hospital*. Your brain feels paralyzed. On the verge of panic, you can think of only three possible topics of conversation.

If you pretend to be interested in Major League
    Baseball, turn to page 2.
If you ask Brian if he likes to watch *General Hospital*,
    turn to page 131.
If you mention that your last boyfriend also drove a
    BMW, turn to page 35.

Three years later, you're sitting in your trailer, eating the arugula and walnut salad that the caterer prepares especially for you every morning. You have more than an hour until makeup and wardrobe, so you pass the time by reading the cover story in the latest issue of *Entertainment Weekly*.

The article describes how two casting agents discovered you while eating cream cheese brownies in a Barnes & Noble coffee shop. ("We took one look at her," Reuben explains, "and we knew we'd found our Marilyn Monroe.") Your body double work in a Brad Pitt-John Cusack action-comedy (a huge flop, by the way) led to a handful of commercials, a few sitcom appearances, and then a bit part in a Nora Ephron comedy. With just ninety seconds of screen time, you managed to steal the entire movie, and critics anointed you a star. Now you find yourself acting alongside huge movie stars like Mike Myers, Cameron Diaz, Denzel Washington, Al Pacino, and Meg Ryan.

Hollywood is a strange place, and you know your fifteen minutes of fame could run out at any moment—so you're banking as much money as possible and just trying to enjoy yourself. The food is good, the weather's terrific, and you never *ever* have trouble getting a date for Friday night!

THE END

You veer onto the mountain bike trail and immediately find yourself plummeting down a steep incline, splashing through a ravine, and smashing over a series of painful bumps. You grab onto the handlebars for dear life, fearing that you're going to be thrown from the bike at any moment.

"I . . . can't . . . hold . . . *onnnnnnn!*" Pete shouts, and then suddenly he's gone.

You squeeze the brakes but can't slow down. At the bottom of the hill, your front tire drops in a ditch; you flip forward over your handlebars and land in a muddy creek. The engine on the motorcycle sputters out. You try standing up, but your right ankle will no longer bear the weight of your body. You must have sprained it, or worse.

You sit there for several minutes, and then the silence is broken by voices. You recognize that it's Pete, and he's pleading with Larry and Joe to spare his life.

It won't be long, you suppose, before you're doing the same thing.

THE END

You knock over your table and hide behind it while bullets and broken glass whiz past you. Another man holding an AK-47 comes charging out of the kitchen, and the shooting finally stops.

"All right," the bearded man shouts. "Now that we have your attention, allow me to introduce myself. My name is Larry DeVito, and I'm robbing this restaurant with my brother, Joe. If everyone does what we ask, I promise that no one will get hurt!"

You look around and realize that, thankfully, all of the customers are still alive—and no one looks hurt. But then you see Pete clutching a bloody wound in his left bicep, and you realize he's been shot. The rabbi is tying a dinner napkin around the wound, to reduce the flow of the blood.

Meanwhile, Joe walks around the restaurant with a large duffel bag, collecting purses, wallets, and cell phones from all of the customers, including you. Larry is standing at the cash register, emptying its contents into a knapsack.

Out on the street, you can hear the sirens of several approaching police cars. It sounds as if things are about to get ugly.

Turn to page 33.

After another twenty minutes of driving, Larry and Joe realize that they're home-free—and they begin congratulating themselves for pulling off another caper. You continue wriggling your wrists, certain now that the cord is getting looser. In another minute or so, you could be out of it altogether.

"Now that you've made a safe getaway," Pete says, "why don't you let us go?"

"Shut up!" Joe tells him. "We'll let you go when we're ready!"

The Grand Marquis plunges deep into a wooded area. There's a very sharp turn coming up; as Larry starts to brake the car, you watch the needle on the speedometer dip below 15.

The wire cord is finally loose enough for you to slip out of. You could open your door, jump out of the car, run to safety, and tell the police that Pete is being taken to a cabin in Fairfield. You could also open your door, jump out of the car, and break your neck. But whatever you do, you have to do it quickly!

If you decide to jump out, turn to page 103.
If you stay with Pete, turn to page 84.

You enter the living room, which has more square footage than all the rooms in your apartment combined. The furniture is tasteful, the walls have artwork, and the bookshelves are filled with real books—no ragged Tom Clancy paperbacks here, just dozens of serious, well-worn volumes on medicine, history, politics, and, of course, baseball. On the mantel above the fireplace are several framed photographs; one of them, you notice, is lying facedown.

Brian is watching you carefully and quickly turns the photograph faceup. "I'm not sure how that fell over." He shrugs. "It's me and my sister."

In the photograph, the woman is dressed in a white wedding gown. Brian wears a tuxedo and corsage, and he's embracing the woman in a hug that literally lifts her off her feet. Before you can ask any questions, Brian's cell phone starts to ring. He checks the display, sighs, and says, "It's the hospital. I'm sorry, but I have to take this call. The bathroom's down the hall, if you want to freshen up."

He steps out onto the balcony and slides the glass door closed, so you won't be able to hear his conversation. You feel as if you're picking up a strange vibe— but then again, maybe you're just being paranoid.

If you decide to leave the apartment and go home, turn to page 55.
If you use his bathroom to freshen up, turn to page 74.

You don't think of Chaz again until six months later, while visiting your little brother at his college dormitory. You haven't been to a campus in years, and you're surprised by how much college has changed. For one thing, plenty of boys seem to notice you. In fact, many of them step forward and introduce themselves. Guys were never so friendly when you were an undergraduate, and you assume they're entranced by your hip, big-city-girl attitude.

But by the end of the day, after you've met more than twenty of your brother's classmates—and after you've signed autographs for three of them—you're convinced something is up. "What's going on with these guys?" you ask.

Your brother shakes his head. "I didn't want to tell you, but here goes." He punches a few buttons on his laptop and opens a webpage called www.showering-sexbabes.com. The headline reads CLICK HERE FOR PHOTOS OF OUR MOST POPULAR SHOWER SEX BABE. Underneath the headline are a dozen different photos of you, rubbing psoriasis shampoo into your breasts while showering at the Samson Hotel.

With a shock, you realize that Chaz really *did* work for an Internet start-up. And in addition to being a fabulous lover, he was also quite good at hiding cameras.

THE END

"We won't survive the rapids," you tell Pete. "I'm steering us toward the calmer water."

You have no trouble navigating the canoe on the straightaway—but it only takes a minute before Larry and Joe catch up to you in their powerboat. In a race on calm water against a gasoline-powered engine, you really didn't have a chance.

Larry aims his gun at Pete. "This is like shooting fish in a barrel," he says.

"Not here on the river," Joe tells him. "Let's bring them back to the cabin, so no one else will hear."

They lift both of you into the powerboat and begin heading back toward the cabin. And since the remaining four minutes and eighteen seconds of your life are rather unpleasant, it's probably best if the story just stops here.

THE END

You move closer and take Pete's hand. "I'd love to have dinner," you tell him, and then Pete leans forward and kisses you. Even after being shot, tied up, almost drowned, and nearly bleeding to death, he's actually a pretty good kisser.

You can't wait to see what he's like tomorrow night.

THE END

"Everything I know about doctors comes from watching *General Hospital*," you tell him. "Did you ever watch that show?"

Brian laughs. "You can't imagine how many people ask me that!" he exclaims. "I grew up with three older sisters, and they were all obsessed with that show. I'd come home from school to watch cartoons, and they'd all be watching Robert Scorpio saving the world. Or Luke and Laura's wedding."

"Laura's dress was so beautiful," you sigh.

There's nothing like old TV shows to spark a discussion, and pretty soon you and Brian are running down a list of your favorite classics: *Diff'rent Strokes, The Facts of Life, Miami Vice, Laverne and Shirley,* and, of course, *Fantasy Island.*

"Welcome to my island," Brian says, in what must be the best impression of Ricardo Montalban you've ever heard, and you both crack up laughing.

Turn to page 80.

When you press Play, the answering machine emits a series of harsh, ear-splitting beeps, like a delivery truck backing into a loading dock. Then the message begins, and you realize the volume is completely maxed out: "HEY, LITTLE BROTHER, IT'S ME. THANKS FOR LETTING ME CRASH AT YOUR PLACE LAST NIGHT." You press every button on the answering machine but can't seem to find a volume switch. You can't even make the message stop. "LISTEN, I LEFT MY MEDS IN YOUR BATHROOM LAST NIGHT. CAN YOU CALL ME WHEN YOU GET HOME? YOU KNOW I'M NOT SUPPOSED TO MISS A DOSE." All you can do is put your hand over the speaker, hoping to muffle the voice as much as possible. "THANKS, BRO—AND LISTEN, YOU NEED TO STOP WORRYING ABOUT LOSING YOUR HAIR. I SAW THOSE FANCY SHAMPOOS IN YOUR SHOWER, AND YOU'RE WASTING YOUR MONEY—"

Suddenly, Brian appears in the doorway with a tall, thin redhead—the same woman from the photograph on the mantel. They realize what you are doing and stare at you in disbelief.

"Who are you?" you ask.

"I'm Elizabeth Anderson, Brian's sister," she says. "Who are you?"

Before you can even answer, Brian raises his hand, cutting you off. "She's nobody," he tells his sister. "And she was just leaving."

THE END

It's another typical morning on Planet Neptune, and you awaken to your usual rituals: a pedicure, a foot massage, chocolate-covered strawberries, and then a bath in the hot springs with three of your loyal subjects. In accordance with your wishes, these subjects assume the physical forms of George Clooney, Denzel Washington, and Russell Crowe.

After your bath, one of the council leaders enters your chamber and reminds you that it's Thursday— and every Thursday, the queen will typically go out on her balcony and make a proclamation to her subjects. Many of these subjects have traveled thousands of miles just to catch a glimpse of their ruler.

You open your balcony and look out on the beautiful Neptune landscape. Thousands of Neptunians have gathered in the courtyard below, and they greet you with thunderous applause. You raise your hands, signaling for them to quiet, but they won't stop clapping. Last week, the cheering lasted for a full twenty minutes. According to Xandor, you are by far the most popular queen in Neptune's history, and you are celebrated everywhere for your kindness, generosity, and wisdom.

Needless to say, it beats a life of bad blind dates on planet Earth.

THE END

About the Author

....

MIRANDA CLARKE lives in Philadelphia and often has difficulty making smart decisions (particularly when faced with a dessert tray). She can be reached via e-mail at mirandaclarke1000@hotmail.com.

About the Illustrator

....

PAMELA HOBBS resides in London and insists that most English people are not like the characters in an Austin Powers film. She can be contacted via her website, www.pamorama.com.

turn to page 83